WINGS OF A DEVIL

A DARK MFM ROMANCE

A SINNERS AND ANGELS NOVELLA

LUNA PIERCE

BLURB

He's the reason my brother is dead, and I will stop at nothing to get revenge.

I'll do anything to end his life, even if it means sleeping with the enemy to get information.

But once I'm up close and personal with the tattooed bad boy I'm fake dating and the dangerous silver fox who murdered my brother, I start to discover things that can't possibly be true.

His death was covered up, but there's much more to the story than I bargained for.

And the more I dig, the more I realize nothing is as it seems.

One thing is certain though: I'm in over my head, and without meaning to, all of our lives—and hearts—are on the line.

following without question. I crash my lips onto his, tasting myself on his tongue. "Fuck me," I mutter against him while reaching down to clench his shaft.

"What's the rush?" He rocks himself in my hand as he trails his back down to my wet slit. Axel dips two of his fingers inside, and I moan in response, my eyes fluttering shut briefly.

"I'm going to be late for work." I steady my gaze on the clock on his bedside table, my heart picking up the pace with antici-pation. His apartment is ten minutes farther than mine from the office I work at, and if I don't leave in the next seven minutes, I won't make it on time.

He might not care about his job, but I can't afford to lose mine.

And considering the rules I've put in place, I won't be coming back tonight if we don't do it now. Not to mention, I have plans that cannot be changed. Plans that might finally take me one step further.

I snag a condom off the table and rip it open with my teeth, sliding the latex over his shaft and positioning him at my entrance.

Axel stares down at me. "You're really pretty, you know that?"

I sigh and roll my eyes, dropping my hand from his cock, defeat washing over me. His massive erection says he wants to fuck, but maybe I've got it all wrong. I slide out from under him and reach for my panties off the floor.

"Oh no you don't." Axel wraps his arm around my waist and drags me onto my back with minimal effort. He pins my hands over my head with one hand and uses the other to line himself up with my hole. "Is this what you want?" His blue gaze intensifies.

"Yes," I pant, a bit out of breath from the shift in dynamic.

He plunges into me, his cock stretching and filling me with both pain and pleasure. "You want it quick, Banks?"

Even the way he says my name is sexy.

Axel fucks me hard and grinds against my pelvic bone with each thrust, my clit enjoying every ounce of the friction. His grip tightens on my hands, not daring to let me free. He drags his other palm over my cheek, his thumb tugging my bottom lip down and his grasp settling around my throat. His tattooed hand no doubt making one seductive necklace. If only I could take a picture to make it last longer.

With my plan so close to completion, my time with Axel will soon come to an end.

I whimper, my core tensing with the nearness of my orgasm. "Tighter."

Axel squeezes the sides of my neck even more, applying just the right amount of pressure to restrict my airway. He slows his rhythm but fucks me deeper, a sly grin forming on his face. "I know, baby, I know."

Whoever taught this man to fuck deserves an award, or at the very least, a forever cold pillow.

Such a shame I have to give him and his delicious cock up. Nothing good ever lasts.

I pinch my eyes shut and revel in the wave seconds away from crashing over me.

"Look at me." He slides his hand from around my throat to tilt my chin up at him.

I open my eyes and stare into those mesmerizing blue orbs before he presses his lips against mine.

His mouth suppresses my moans as I quiver around him. Axel's climax follows only seconds behind my own. His motion comes to a halt, and he rests his forehead on mine. "Fuck, Banks."

I smile with an exhale. "That we did." Out of instinct, I press another kiss on his lips. "I have to get to work, Axel."

"Right." He climbs off of me and collapses next to my body, his forearm landing over his head. "I have a meeting, too."

I slide my arms through the straps of my bra and secure it in place, raising an eyebrow and glancing back at him. "Yeah, who with?"

He ignores my question. "You want to get dinner tonight?"

"I already have plans." I finish putting my clothes on. "We're still on for Friday though."

At this, he removes his arm and reaches over to pull me toward him. He kisses the section of my side that's exposed when my shirt rides up. "You have a hot date?"

"Maybe," I laugh and ruffle his long-ish dark hair. "You jealous?"

"A little, but there's no one man who could ever be good enough for you." He releases me and lies back, propping himself up to gawk at me as I finish getting dressed. "A woman like you needs a whole army of men."

I raise my brow. "You know one that's accepting applications?" I slide my clutch off the dresser and shove my half-charged phone inside. With my back still to him, I ask the question he didn't answer again. "Who's your meeting with?" After all, this whole thing is about gathering information.

"Savini." The single name from his lips freezes me in place.

My heart thuds, and I force myself to act fucking normal.

Savini.

The man who killed my brother.

CHAPTER TWO

I take a final look at myself in the mirror, smoothing out the flyaways from my burnt orange hair. I tuck it behind my shoulders then decide against it, letting it fall wherever it wants before touching up the bright red lipstick on my lips.

"You've got this," I reassure my reflection.

A couple walks past me and into the restaurant belonging to this swanky hotel.

I follow them in, not too closely, and smile politely at the hostess that greets me.

"Party of one?" She reaches for a menu.

"Actually," I say. "I'll sit at the bar, if that's okay?"

"Of course." She motions for me to help myself and turns her attention to the group that walked in after me.

My heels click against the floor with each step, drowning out the sound of my thundering heart. In all the time I've spent on my mission for revenge, I've never been quite this close to my target. That is, if my intel was correct and he's here at all. There's a significant possibility that I'm not as good at sleuthing as I think I am.

I guess I'll know soon enough.

With my limited options, I settle into a seat as far as possible from the entrance, near the wall, where I can have a decent vantage point to keep an eye on things.

The barkeep, a sweet-faced older woman, approaches. She lays a napkin in front of me and asks, "What can I get for you, sweetheart?"

"Martini, dirty, please." I could have probably chosen a drink with a little less punch, but I need something to calm my nerves quickly and a martini will do just the trick.

"Would you like to start a tab or put it on your room?"

I slide my debit card out of my clutch and hand it to her. "A tab will be fine." There's no telling how long I'll be sitting here, and I can't sip on one drink all night. I'll have to pick something that's not as potent next time, though.

She takes the piece of plastic and walks away, going to work on setting up my tab and making my drink. She holds out her finger to a tall, thin man that approaches. "I'll be right with you."

Another patron, a guy sitting two chairs to my left, keeps obnoxiously looking at me like he's either trying to get my attention or is completely unaware that I have peripheral vision and can see him gawking at me.

I roll my eyes, sighing, and turn to him, an opening that I will no doubt regret.

He hops off his chair and slithers onto the one next to mine, sliding his drink along the top of the bar. He holds out his hand. "Colton."

I glance down at his clammy palm, but don't take it. "Banks." I pause and add, "Mild germaphobe." It's not entirely a lie.

"Right, yeah." Colton hesitates and then lowers his arm. He brings his mug to his lips, some of the condensation dripping onto his pants in the process. Does this guy realize that not a single thing he's doing is attractive? "So, you like it dirty?"

I narrow my gaze at him, very much one of those *looks-could-kill* moments. "Excuse me?"

He swallows another gulp of his beer and wipes at his mouth with his finger, then points it at the new arrival sitting in front of me. "Your martini. Did I hear you order it dirty?"

I blink to try to erase the awkwardness I just created. "Yeah." I sip the potent cocktail. "Olive juice." Here I thought he was attempting to be a perv when he was only asking about my drink.

"Cool." He fiddles with the handle on his mug of golden beer and turns his attention back to me. "You come here often?"

Really? That's the line he's going to use?

"No." I scan the faces behind him, and at the random people sitting at the tables. None of them looking any more familiar than the last.

"Can I buy you a drink?" Colton straightens his shoulders like he's going to somehow persuade me with better posture. His plain face and off-the-rack suit do him no favors, the material nowhere near the size he should be wearing. It's like he's playing dress-up in his father's clothing.

"I have a drink." I point to the beverage I had only taken one sip of.

"I could get you another," he suggests. "Whatever you want." He raises his hand to signal to the lady but I raise mine and press his down. So much for avoiding physical contact.

"I'm okay. Thank you, though."

He's just trying to be a nice guy, Banks. Don't be so hard on him.

But the second I attempt to cut him the slightest bit of slack, he dares to lean in close and place his slimy palm on my thigh. "It's *one* drink, come on." His gaze turns from soft to hardened, like a darker version of this man could appear at any moment.

"Remove your hand from my leg," I say through gritted teeth, my stare focused on him, my hand slowly creeping toward my clutch on the bar, where a knife is tucked inside.

Stabbing a random dude in this upscale bar wasn't my idea of how this night would go, but if I've learned anything in all my years, it's that sometimes you have to fight fire with fire. Another day, another bar, another innocent girl won't have the chance to stand up for herself, and when that day comes, I want this fucking creep to remember the fierce redhead that shoved a knife into his thigh. I want to be the reason he questions ever laying a hand on someone else ever again.

But before I can react, a large figure latches onto Colton's throat, picking him up from his seat and slamming him into the bar.

With their hand still tightly around Colton's neck, they look over at me. "Are you okay?"

"Y-y-yeah." I stare up at the man's face, in awe at seeing it so up close and personal.

A scar trails his forehead, across his eye, and down to his cheek. Dark, brown eyes, the color deep enough to be mistaken for black. A five-o-clock shadow speckled with salt and pepper shades. He's more beautiful than I imagined he'd be, and that alone sends my heart rate through the roof.

"Do you know this man?" the gorgeous older man asks me.

"No," I say, my voice barely a whisper.

He turns his attention to Colton, who has his hands wrapped around this guy's forearm, desperate to pry himself free of his hold.

My gaze flits around the room, noticing how no one pays us a significant amount of attention. Even the barkeep goes about her business and fills a customer's mug with draft beer.

Shouldn't someone do something? Clearly, Colton is being assaulted, but not a single person comes to his defense.

The man grips Colton's neck tighter and leans in. "You do not touch what is not yours. You do not step foot in this bar, this hotel, on this fucking side of town, ever again. And if you ever lay a finger on another woman without her consent, I will fucking hunt you down and gut you like the pig you are. Do you fucking hear me?"

My eyes go wide, my heart pattering harder and harder.

Colton nods despite being pinned into place, tears trickling down both of his cheeks.

The man shoves Colton to the side and straightens his own jacket. "Get the fuck out of here before I change my mind."

Colton scurries off, tripping over chairs and customers as he frantically tries to get away as quickly as possible.

Finally, like a fucking eternity later, the man turns around to face me. "Are you okay?" His voice is thick and gravely, but with a sort of strange smoothness to it.

I blink, once, then twice. This can't be real. This can't be happening.

"Are you here with someone?" he asks when I don't say anything.

Slowly, I shake my head back and forth.

He points to my martini. "Is that yours?"

Even slower, I bob my head up and down. Is this what I've diminished to—non-verbal communication?

"Rosita," he raises his voice to call out to the barkeep. "Put that on my tab." He latches onto my drink, holding it with a bizarre gentleness despite his recent exchange with Colton. "Come with me."

Against my better judgment, I stand, following him away from the bar and into a little corner booth that's tucked away from prying eyes, but gives him the perfect view of everyone in this place. It's no wonder I hadn't noticed him yet, he was in my blind spot. But to him, he must have witnessed my every move from the second I stepped foot in here.

"Have you eaten?" He motions for me to sit, then slides into the spot across from me. "Forgive me, I haven't introduced myself." He extends his hand, the same one that was wrapped around Colton's throat only moments prior. "Savini. Lorenzo Savini."

A laugh bubbles up and out of my chest. "I'm sorry." I clasp my palm over my mouth but then remove it to place it in his. "The way you said it, it reminded me of *'Bond, James Bond.'*" I enunciate the words like I'm imitating a man's voice. How did I go from not saying a word to mocking him? Not exactly the best way to start this interaction. But I guess him almost murdering a man for touching me isn't ideal either.

Nor was it expected. Savini is the man that killed my brother, but now he's also the man that defended my honor and saved me from having to stab a dude in public. The outcome of the latter no doubt causing much more trouble than what he had done. The people in this place seem to collectively fear Savini, which only confirms what I already suspected of him.

He's a bad man. A killer. A criminal. Him coming to my aid doesn't change that.

"A few similarities maybe, but I'd like to think I dress better." Savini adjusts his cufflinks.

I bring my martini glass to my lips and chug the entirety of the contents.

Savini raises a brow. "She's thirsty." He places a finger in the air to summon a waiter, and a second later, one appears.

"Another martini for the lady."

"Actually," I cut him off. "Can I have a Michter's Rye, neat? Please."

Savini interjects. "Pull a bottle of rye from my reserve. And…" He studies me for a second. "Are you a vegetarian?"

"No."

He turns his attention back to the waiter. "Same thing I'm having for dinner, bring them out at the same time. That will be all for now."

The waiter leaves without another word and Savini drains the rest of his drink. "You never told me your name."

"You never asked." The words slip out more arrogant than I mean for them to, but with the liquid courage now coursing through my veins, I'm back to my more confident self.

The corner of Savini's lip twitches like he might smile, but he doesn't. "Fair enough." He tilts his head slightly. "I shall call you…fawn."

"Fawn?" I lean forward, crossing my arms and resting my elbows on the table.

"Mmhm." Savini mimics my move and stares right at me. "Walking in here completely unaware of the attention you're commanding. Might as well be a deer waltzing into a lion's den." His gaze doesn't leave mine. "Men these days don't understand respect, let alone consent. A beautiful butterfly like you, they'll pluck your wings one by one until there's nothing left. It's not safe out there for you."

"And you think I'm safe here, with you?" I swallow the lump forming in my throat. Savini has no idea that I know the truth about who he is—the man that murders innocent people for a living.

At this, a sly grin finally forms on his face. "Oh, I'm the worst of them all."

"Then why did you interject yourself earlier?" If he's such a bad guy, why would he care about what some fuck boy is doing?

"He needed to be dealt with."

"And you think I couldn't handle myself?" I clench my jaw, unsure why I'm so fucking defensive. Oh wait, probably because this is the same man that killed my brother in cold blood.

"I never said that."

I part my lips to speak but am interrupted by the waiter returning with a bottle for the table. He holds it out to Savini and waits for his approval.

Savini takes it and the two glasses in the waiter's other hand and then waves him away.

"That's not what I ordered," I tell Savini.

"No, but it's better." He pulls the cork out of the bottle and pours two knuckles worth into both glasses. Savini nudges one toward me. "A toast."

"To what?"

"Never being underestimated."

I clink my glass against his and take a cautious sip of the amber liquid. "Mmm." I allow myself to indulge a bit more before setting the cup back on the table. "This tastes expensive."

"But not everything that is expensive tastes good, don't forget that." Savini winks at me, and it's everything I can do to not drive the knife tucked in my clutch into his chest.

He might have influence, power, and devilishly good looks, but he's a monster and it's up to me to make him pay. It's just a matter of time until the opportunity presents itself, and I can finally see this plan come to fruition.

When I came here tonight, I never anticipated I would get this close to him. Maybe near him, but not sharing a pricey bottle of rye and sitting right across from his deceiving beautiful face.

"Just ask and get it over with." His statement catches me off guard, like everything else that's happened tonight.

"What?" The confusion on my face is genuine.

"This." He runs his finger along his scar.

"Oh, I wasn't…" I noticed it earlier, I mean, who wouldn't, but that wasn't what was on my mind now.

"You don't have to lie." His serious stare bores into me.

"I'm not lying." But since I can't exactly tell him the actual truth, I take the bait. "You can tell me if you want to, but you don't have to."

"My dad." He leans back, bringing his cup to his lips. Savini tips the entire contents in his mouth and swallows harshly. "Tried to kill me when I was ten. Almost succeeded." He drops the glass onto the table and swirls the empty thing around.

Holy fuck.

"I'm sorry." I'm not sure why I say it. But there's something about the idea of a child being hurt by someone who should have been there to protect them that makes my resolve soften for this man. He might not deserve my sympathy but ten-year-old Lorenzo does. And maybe that's who the apology is for, not this dangerous man sitting in front of me.

"It was a lifetime ago." Savini pours more of the rye into his glass, and then, without asking, fills mine, too.

My heart aches for the child of his past that was brutally attacked by his father. A sort of compassion that only someone who had an abusive parent can have fills me, and my mind swirls with memories I've repressed for many years. Memories that haunt me in my dreams and plague my waking life. One's that I've mastered shoving into the depths of my psyche.

"Penny for your thoughts?" Savini draws my attention toward him.

I meet his gaze, unsure of what to say. A part of me wants to tell him who I am, who he is to me, and confess that I've been stalking him for the past six months in an attempt to uncover the truth about my brother's murder. To tell him that I never bought the story that the police gave me, and that the double homicide in that alley beside Bram's diner was nothing more than a big fucking cover-up. The media may have bought it but I didn't.

But instead, I tell him another truth. "No kid deserves that from a parent."

We stare at each other for a long moment, almost like a standoff of sorts.

Luckily, the waiter arrives with our food, saving us both from having to continue such a growingly awkward conversation. I may have been tracking him for half a year but we've only known each other all of fifteen minutes.

"Can I get you anything else, sir?" The waiter stands there anxiously.

Savini waves him away and nods toward my plate. "Hope you're hungry."

I settle my sights on the perfectly cooked filet, steaming chunks of seasoned potatoes, and roasted broccolini. My stomach growls in response, alerting me to the lunch I skipped while I was busy summarizing the depositions for work. Being a new associate essentially means being a partner's bitch. They don't really tell you that in school. A cruel reality you figure out after countless skipped meals and endless hours of overtime to make everything perfect while your boss sips fancy wine at meetings with executives or doing whatever overpaid partners do.

The waiter returns a moment later, sliding my debit card toward me and leaving without another word.

I finish chewing the juicy piece of steak and swallow before saying, "I'm paying for my meal."

Savini shakes his head and wipes his mouth with his napkin. "Not necessary."

"I insist." Scoring free food might be a perk to my normal relationship situations, but that isn't what this is about with Savini. Being frugal has nothing to do with getting revenge.

"Listen, fawn." Savini takes another swig of his rye. "It's been a while since I've enjoyed the company I've kept during a meal. You're doing me a favor, really. Please don't ruin it by bringing up the patriarchy."

"The patriarchy?" I grin and sip my own drink. "You almost murdered a guy for touching me. That has male dominance written all over it."

"Times are changing, but some things should remain the same."

"Are you about to mansplain this to me?"

"Would you prefer another form of communication?" Savini winks and manages to completely throw me off-kilter.

A million dirty thoughts run through my mind but I follow

each of them up with the reminder that this strangely charismatic man is the same one who killed my brother.

I shouldn't, but I find myself wanting to tell him the real reason why I'm here. If him attacking Colton was any indication, he could probably kill me right here and now and get away with it, every person in this place looking the other way as my death is covered up just like Jared's was. Only no one will look into my death the way I did his.

The way I found out that Jared was working for some man named Franklin—that he was an errand boy for a criminal mastermind, and his death was ordered by Franklin and executed by the man sitting in front of me. I might not be able to take down Franklin, but Savini is another story.

It's amazing what information a pretty face and showing some skin can get you. It wasn't long before I weaseled my way into Axel's life, the closest connection I had found to Savini was eating out of the palm of my hand. I just had to listen closely and pay attention to figure out where Savini would be and when. This place was the most public of them all, although I didn't expect to get a private audience the first time I crossed paths with the mercenary who murdered my brother.

Killing Savini and avenging Jared's death becomes more of a reality with each passing second.

CHAPTER THREE

"You. Look. Incredible." Axel extends his arm, twirling me around in a circle before pulling me in.

I giggle against his chest, something strangely genuine about it despite the entire façade of this whole situation.

Being with Axel has never been difficult. Not a single moment of our time together has felt forced, but I couldn't help myself from enjoying it even though I knew it would never last. It couldn't even if I wanted it to.

"Thanks." I straighten his shirt collar and smooth out the wrinkles. "You're not so bad yourself."

Axel's fitted black button-down hugs his shoulders in all the right places. The few buttons undone at the top tease his tattooed chest, and his sleeves are rolled up just enough to show off more ink-stained skin. His matching onyx slacks accentuate his ass well. His entire aesthetic could be something out of a GQ magazine. Definitely a Pinterest-worthy bad boy.

He draws the attention of both men and women alike, but his gaze remains trained on only me.

Violet waves at me from across the way, her blonde hair

bouncing around her shoulders with each step she takes toward us. "I am so jealous." She pulls me in for a quick embrace, kissing both of my cheeks and then reaching for Axel. "You two are fucking adorable." Violet clutches her chest. "It seriously hurts. Now tell me, where can I find one?" She exaggerates and scans the crowd. "Male or female, you know I'm not picky."

"You are a vision, V." I latch onto her hand and weave my fingers through hers. "And if I played ball for both teams, you'd be my first pick."

She grins and shakes her head. "Did you just make a sports reference?"

I laugh. "It was terrible wasn't it?"

Violet nods. "Yes, please don't do that ever again."

"You two can catch up while I get you drinks. Your usuals?" Axel looks from me to Violet and then back at me.

"Thanks, lover boy." Violet unclasps her clutch, pulls out a mirror, and fixes her lipstick. "You sure I look okay?"

"What's got you all insecure?" I cross my arms over my chest and narrow my gaze at her. "Who do I need to kill?"

Violet bites at her bottom lip and shrugs. "This is the first big thing I've been to since..."

"Nope." I cut her off. "Don't even say his name. He's not worth your breath." I grip her shoulders and stare into her beautiful hazel eyes. "You are fucking gorgeous. Do you hear me? You are worthy of so much more than that shit bag had to offer. He was lucky you gave him the time of day, and any man, or woman, who dares to enter your life should be fucking honored you paid them any attention. Hell, V, I'm blessed you even like me. Seriously. You're my best friend, and I'm not joking when I say I will gut anyone who hurts you ever again."

At this, Violet smiles. "But then I'd have to help you hide the body, and that could be a lot of work, you know?"

"We'd figure it out, we always do."

A figure appears from behind me. At first, I expect it to be

Axel, but it's his voice that gives him away. Thick, gravely, that seductive swagger embedded in every word. "Body disposal. I could be of assistance."

Lorenzo Savini.

He extends his well-manicured hand toward Violet. "Lorenzo."

Violet slides her palm into his, completely unaware of how dangerous the man in front of her is. "Violet." She nods at me. "And this is Banks."

Savini's cheek curls upward as he moves from Violet to me. "Banks, what a pleasure."

To Violet, Savini is meeting us both for the first time, but he and I know the truth. Only, why he goes along with it is beyond me.

Lies upon lies upon lies.

"Babe." Axel appears at my side with drinks in hand. When his gaze moves from the cups in his grasp to the man standing next to me, his mouth falls open.

Violet completely ignores the shock written on Axel's ruggedly handsome face and introduces the two of them. "Axel, this is Lorenzo, Lorenzo, this is Axel."

Axel passes me a drink, then Violet, freeing his hand to put it in Savini's. "What are you doing here?"

The two of them shake hands longer than necessary, tension rising between them and their firm grips on each other.

"It's a charity event." Savini stares at Axel. "And I'm a rather charitable man."

"Aw, that's sweet." Violet continues to overlook the weirdness of the situation. "What are you bidding on tonight?"

Savini side-eyes me. "I haven't decided yet. I hear there are law services offered by a local firm. I could use some legal advice."

The package my employer roped me into giving away. Two hours of my time because people would be willing to bid on it with the firm's name attached to it, but the actual partners wouldn't have to do shit for work. Another one of the many pitfalls of being a first-year associate. I expected some start-up or hedge fund brat to bid on it, not the fucking enemy.

"Oh my God, Banks is your girl." Violet takes a sip of her long island iced tea. "She's the smartest, really. I wouldn't be surprised if she's being head-hunted as we speak."

Axel releases Savini and throws his arm over my shoulder, pulling me toward him. "How's your drink, babe?"

I tip the thing back, downing the contents in one fell swoop. I slide the olive off the stick and into my mouth. "Great. Thanks."

Between Savini and I lying about knowing each other, Savini and Axel lying about knowing each other, and me lying to Axel about our entire relationship, I grow unsure of how the fuck to move forward. I thought I had a handle on all of this but it's like everything was tossed aside when I ran into Savini in that bar.

Now, I don't know which way is up or how to continue on this dangerous path I'm on.

Savini takes the empty cup from me. "How about we get you another drink?" He latches onto my arm and tugs me away. Axel grips me tighter but ends up releasing me, no doubt not wanting to cause such a public scene.

"I'll be right back," I tell my best friend and fake boyfriend. I free myself from Savini but go along with him. "Why did you act like we didn't know each other?"

He raises his brow and glances over at me. "Why did you?"

I sigh and lean against the bar, waiting for one of the overly busy bartenders to come over to us. The second Savini approaches, so does a young man. "Two of your finest ryes."

He turns toward me, his stature towering over me. He's probably the same height as Axel, but there's something different about his masculine energy. It's more mature, some-thing that naturally comes with the massive age difference between us. Axel is sexy and handsome, whereas Savini has this sort of sophisticated vibe that can only be attributed to many additional years of experience. His stare is dangerous but alluring, making being near him that much more exhilarating.

"What do you see in him?" Savini doesn't look away, not even when the bartender returns with our drinks.

"Thank you," I tell the guy for the both of us.

"I asked you a question," Savini says through gritted teeth.

"Why do you care?" I bring my glass to my lips and sip the golden liquid.

"You're playing a risky game, fawn. You don't know what kind of people you're messing with. Sooner or later, you're going to get hurt."

"Is that supposed to scare me?" I step closer, tilting my head up at him. "I'm not afraid of you."

His breath caresses my cheek, his gaze lingering on my lips for a second too long. "You should be terrified."

A chill runs up my spine, speckling my flesh with goosebumps. Heat builds between my legs, betraying my every emotion. I shouldn't feel this way. I fucking hate him. And yet, the thought of him bending me over this bar is enough to make my face flush red.

Axel and Violet rescue me from my rampant mind.

"Let's dance." Axel's warm hand latches onto mine. I quickly down the rest of my drink and leave the glass on the counter and Savini behind. Maybe Axel's tight body pressed along mine paired with the alcohol coursing through me will rid me of my sinful visions.

But the second I'm glued to the tatted criminal, our bodies swaying together with ease, I can't help but think about Savini pushing up on me from behind.

What the fuck is wrong with me?

Axel's voice distracts me temporarily. "He's bad news, Banks."

The melody turns slow, and I sigh and move to the unhurried rhythm with him. "So are you." I grin at him, both of us knowing very well that he's no angel either.

Axel shakes his head. "No. I'm well aware I don't deserve you, but him, Banks, he'll eat you up and spit you out. You don't belong in his world." He tucks a strand of my copper hair behind my ear and runs his thumb along my cheek. "Listen, I know we said we weren't exclusive, and I don't expect that to change but for me, it's you. It's always been you. I can't control who you see or what you do, but I'm warning you. Not for any reason other than I care about you. Okay?"

My gut twists. The lies build up on top of each other, a weight that grows heavier with each passing moment. How can I continue to do this to Axel when his intentions seem so... pure? I went into this with one thing on my mind—revenge. Does Axel really deserve to get caught in the crossfire?

A pale, thin woman approaches and gently touches my shoulder. "They're ready for you, Banks."

"Promise me we'll talk about this later?" Axel lets me go, his fingers holding on as our bodies are separated.

My heart aches for the doomed possibilities. Once he finds out the truth, he'll hate me for what I've done. His feelings will turn to ash and all that will be left of us is betrayal. I knew the risks when I approached him that dreary night at a dive bar, hair sticking to my cheeks and my clothes soaked from the rain. It wasn't how I planned our meet-cute to go, but I used my inopportune circumstances to bait him into feeling sorry for the stranded, lost girl who needed help. I knew exactly where I was, and what I was doing, only I hadn't accounted for the random thunderstorm that sent me seeking shelter. I could have asked any of the other patrons for assistance, even gotten a ride-share and come up with another plan later, but I knew if I didn't act, I would have backed out and never followed through with any of this. The thirst for revenge fueling me every step of the way.

"This way." The event coordinator leads me up a few steps and motions for me to walk out onto the brightly lit stage.

I squint to avoid the excessive canned lighting and come to a stop beside a lady standing at the microphone in the center of the landing. I only manage to catch the very end of her spiel.

"...With a 4.0-grade point average from Stanford University, please welcome Banks Manor from Briar & Connor." The lady clears her throat. "Can we start the bidding at five hundred dollars?"

No freaking way someone is going to pay that much money for two hours of my legal time. I should have known this whole thing was stupid when my boss insisted I do it. I should have pushed, told him to do it himself, but I was too afraid he'd fire my ass just for talking back. Sometimes, and I mean very rarely, I know when to keep my mouth shut.

"Five hundred to the gentleman in the back. Do we have six? Six! Do we have seven?"

"Two thousand!" I hear Axel call out from his spot in the corner.

My heart does a flip as I try to make him out through the blaring lights blasting me in the face. Finally, my sights settle on him, a smug grin on his face.

I smile back and shake my head. I guess if I have to spend my time with any of these people, I'd rather it be him, even if I should probably spend those minutes telling him the truth.

"Ten!" another voice calls out.

"Sir, did I hear you correctly? Ten thousand dollars is your bid?"

I scan the crowd until I find the culprit. *Lorenzo Savini.* I'm not entirely sure why I'm surprised, and yet, I am.

He nods his approval, and I bite at the inside of my lip. There's no way Axel will outbid him, and even if he did, I could never allow him to pay that much money just to win whatever pissing match they're currently having.

"Twenty." Axel stands taller, not backing down from Savini's display of masculinity.

A collective gasp fills the room, followed by only the sound of the crackling from the speakers.

"Fifty thousand," Savini says like he's not bidding my entire salary for the year.

Instead of silence, the crowd cheers, applause overpowering the thunderous pulse of my heart.

Fifty. Thousand. Dollars.

Is he fucking insane?

I meet his gaze, both somehow wild and steady all the same time.

Yeah, he's crazy, that much is true, but so am I.

CHAPTER FOUR

"You don't have to go through with this," Axel pleads with me over the phone. "I can contact the venue and see if I can buy out his bid."

I sigh, shifting my cell from one side to the other, pinching it between my face and shoulder. "It's a legally binding contract, Axel."

"There has to be something I can do." Axel's voice is strained.

"It's fine, really. You worry too much."

"And you don't worry enough." He pauses and adds, "I wasn't joking, Banks, he's a bad man. You don't know the things he's done."

But isn't that why I'm in this situation after all? Because I know the truth about Lorenzo Savini and how he killed my brother. Shot and left for dead in an alley. Staged to look like a double homicide gone wrong. He and his friend were casualties in a war they were never going to escape from. How many other innocent lives has Savini ended for a paycheck?

"Then tell me, Axel, otherwise, I have to get off here and finish the case documents before Larry gets back from lunch."

"I can't, Banks. It's for your own safety. The less you know, the better."

"I'll talk to you later, okay?"

Defeat washes over him with an exaggerated sigh. "Promise me you'll be careful?"

"I could ask the same of you." I straighten, pulling the phone into my hand and saying my final goodbye. I toss the thing onto my cluttered desk and rummage through the paperwork to find the fucking folder I swear I was holding two minutes ago. Only now, it's lost in the endless chaos that is my desk. One of these days I'll come up with a better organizational system, but the last thing I want to do when I come up for air between long projects is organize my fucking desk. I'd rather go to the bar and drown my sorrows in cheap dirty martinis with Violet. Or, if I'm lucky, I'll outgrow my fear of asking for help and actually delegate to the underpaid paralegal working in our office.

Fat fucking chance.

I'm ducking under my desk, digging through a stack of shit on the floor when my door creaks open. "Larry, I'm going to need another hour to get things together."

"Is that a pet name?" His voice pierces through me, stopping me dead in my tracks.

Slowly, I collect myself and face him. "What are you doing here?"

"It's nice to see you, too." Savini strolls into my office. His presence is enough to suffocate me right here and now. He fingers the generic artwork lining the wall, and then my framed degree. "Did you really get a 4.0?"

I cross my arms over my chest. "Don't think I have it in me?"

He turns, slowly, and continues to approach. "What did I say about never being underestimated?" Savini stops in front of me, his stare locked onto mine. "I believe you owe me two hours. I'm here to collect."

My eyes widen and I glance down at the shitstorm scattered across my desk. "I'm kind of in the middle of something."

"I figured." He shuffles some of the paperwork mindlessly and then turns his attention back to me. "I'll send a car for you. Say...five o'clock?"

"Today?" I motion to the overly business clothes I'm wearing. "I..." I stop myself when I realize this is perfectly appropriate attire for conducting a legal meeting. But not when I'm trying to seduce the man I want to kill.

"My driver will bring you a change of clothes."

"You want to play dress up? Is that it? You think I'm some doll you get to play with because you were the highest bidder?" Each word comes out of my mouth sassier than the one before it. If we weren't in such a conspicuous place, I wouldn't be surprised by him snatching me by the hair and dragging me out of here kicking and screaming—taking what is rightfully his because he can.

But he doesn't. He remains eerily calm and collected, somehow more terrifying than if he were to do the former.

"Is that what you'd like to do?" Savini doesn't wait for me to answer. "Five o'clock, fawn. If you aren't here, I will find you." He gives me one last penetrating stare before leaving me here, breathless and alone, his final words a threat that haunts me long after he's gone.

⸺☠⸺

I mindlessly finish my work, despite wishing like hell I could distract myself with the tedious tasks I do daily. Instead, I find my gaze flickering to the clock on the wall every so often, seconds creeping by agonizingly slow and way too damn fast all at the same time. The hour hand clicks over onto the five, the sound so quiet yet it rumbles straight through me.

The front door to the office opens, and after a moment of muffled words with the receptionist, a man appears in my doorway.

He holds out a long black garment bag. "Compliments of sir Savini." He hangs it on the hook on the back of my door. "I'll be waiting for you outside, madame."

"You can call me Banks," I blurt out. "No need for such formalities here."

"Thank you, Miss Banks." He nods. "I'm Henry. If you need anything, don't hesitate to ask." Henry leaves my office and exits the same way he came.

A moment later, the receptionist, a sweet-faced young woman named Dani, comes in. "Hey, Banks, I'm cutting out for the day. Do you need anything?" She eyeballs the garment bag. "Oh, what's in there? Hot date?"

I huff and stand, going over to the thing and unzipping it. "No, meeting with that charity event winner." *A man I intend on killing.*

"Wow. In *that*?" Dani skims her finger along the intricate lace lining the dark red dress.

Sitting at the bottom of the bag are a pair of Louboutin heels and a robin egg blue box. That familiar shade most women know and most guys hate. Overpriced jewelry was never my thing, but when I open it to find a rose gold bangle with diamonds, the little girl heart in me flutters at seeing something so damn pretty.

"Holy shit, you know that's a twenty-two-thousand-dollar bracelet, right?"

I blink up at the gawking receptionist. "What?"

Her head bobs up and down. "Yep." Dani fumbles inside the bag to pull out another pale blue box. She opens it and holds it out to me. "And this was nineteen last time I was on their website. Although..." She sighs and takes in its beauty. "It was sold out."

"How do you know all this?"

She glances down at her bare left hand. "I've been dropping hints to Charles every chance I get. The man is oblivious." Dani leans against the doorframe. "This guy, he's got it bad."

And pretty soon, he's going to regret ever laying his sights on me.

———❖———

"Where are we going?" I knock on the hard divider separating Henry and me in this stuffy car. I figured it would only be a short drive to wherever Savini was wanting to meet, but almost thirty minutes later, I realize this might have all been a mistake.

I should have known getting into a random car, wearing an outfit more expensive than I could ever afford, and meeting a dangerous man was a bad idea. This was supposed to be on my terms. A calculated risk, not some stupid rendezvous I had no control over. How am I going to kill him—and get away with it —if I'm allowing him to stack the deck against me?

A voice comes over the speaker. "Miss Banks, we will be arriving shortly."

I open my clutch, confirming for roughly the fifty-seventh time that the things I packed are still in there.

The car slows until it finally stops. I reach for the handle but the door doesn't open. Half a minute passes and Henry's kind face greets me. He reaches for my hand to help me out onto the sidewalk.

I take in my sights, unfamiliar with my surroundings. The street is relatively quiet, with only a few people passing here and there. Another car pulls up behind us but I focus on the entrance to the hotel I'm standing in front of.

Anna Del Sol.

The man standing near the door opens it wide and Savini

steps through to greet me. "You made it." He continues over, reaching out toward me. "Come, fawn."

Henry keeps his head low, not making direct eye contact with Savini.

I offer him a quick parting wave and watch as he nods only slightly in response.

That minimal interaction doesn't exactly make me feel all warm and fuzzy, considering I have no idea where I am. Savini could very well have all these people fearing him to the point that they would turn a blind eye if he were to kidnap me.

I did not fucking think this through.

We walk through another set of double doors, opened by people who pay us no attention other than waiting on Savini hand and foot. If he were to sneeze, I wonder if someone would rush over to pat his nose. The thought is as foolish as thinking I'm going to make it out of this alive. This ignorant deer really has walked straight into the lion's den. That doesn't mean I won't go down without a fight.

"You haven't said a word," Savini glances down at me. His hand rests on mine, which lays on top of his forearm as he guides me through this place.

"A word." I slide myself free and continue walking by his side. I might be in over my head but I can damn well walk without his assistance. This isn't a date, there's no need for him to be a gentleman. But the second my sass kicks in, I remember that I have to play the part if I want this to work. Why is this all so much easier with Axel?

Maybe because Axel isn't the one who murdered my brother.

I check my phone screen, noting the time and the lack of any cell service. "Your two hours started when I stepped out of that car."

We go into an elaborate dining area, the few patrons in the place trailing their gaze over us when we stroll by and through another door. We end up in a private, dimly lit room. Candles line the exterior walls, and there's a few of them on the small table in the center of the space.

"Fair enough." Savini pulls out my seat and motions for me to sit. "I'm pleased to see my design choices were suitable."

"Did I really have a choice?" I lay my clutch on the table and scoot myself closer.

"You always have a choice, even if it doesn't seem like it."

There's something strange about that entire statement. Everything he does is cocky and dominant, leaving me pushed into a corner with everything he does. But, after all, I'm the person who wanted to be in this position. Fate really did me a favor with this one.

"How does your boyfriend feel about being outbid?" Savini unbuttons his suit jacket and settles into his chair across from me.

"He's not my boyfriend."

Savini tilts his head. "Does he know that?"

I chuckle. "He's aware."

I never really was fond of labels. I've always found them to be unbearably suffocating. My therapist probably attributes that to childhood trauma and my fear of commitment. *Whatever.* I never did like paying hundreds of dollars an hour to be told I'm defective.

Savini goes to work pulling the top off a brand-new bottle of rye, and fills two cups, mine first, then his. "Tell me something about you."

"I thought we were here to discuss legal matters?" I carefully sip the rye, not wanting to consume too much too soon. I have to be here for nearly two hours, I can't afford to get sloppy in the first ten minutes, even if what I really want is to drain every drop of the honey-colored decadence into my mouth. He, on the other hand, can drink up. The more intoxicated he becomes, the more information I can get from him.

"Do we have client confidentiality?" Savini matches my pace, only drinking a sip of his rye.

Shit. Is that how things are going to go? At this rate, he'll never even get buzzed.

A waiter appears through a swinging door that must go to the kitchen with two small plates in his grasp. "Your first course, a smoked trout filled with goat cheese and roasted fig."

The second he leaves, I stare at the small, beautiful creation in front of me, then to the man across the way. "How many courses?"

His lips tug back, almost like he wants to smile, but he doesn't. Savini does that a lot. The *almost but not quite.* It's like he's determined to look as miserable as possible at all times.

"How many?" I repeat.

"Twelve."

My eyes widen, my stomach happy but my mind spinning with the lengths he's gone through to impress me tonight. That's what this is, him trying to flaunt his influence? If only he knew the lengths I've gone through to get to him.

"And we're going to get through that in two hours?"

Savini shrugs, not bothered by the time restraint. "It won't if you continue to question everything."

I shove the entire hunk of trout into my mouth, intending to scarf it down quickly, but the second the flavors melt together, I let out a small moan and savor the rest of it. "Damn, that's good." I wipe my lips and wash the food down with some rye.

"Perhaps you could taste your next course instead of swallowing it whole."

I stare at him a moment too long, his last few words—*swallowing it whole*—lingering for what seems like an eternity between us.

Savini raises one of his bushy eyebrows. "Something you'd like to share with the class?"

Yeah, the fact that I don't know which I want more: to kill you or fuck you. Both, sitting high on my list of priorities.

How is it possible to want someone so badly when you hate them so much?

"I'm still waiting on you to tell me something about yourself." I change the subject from anything but the raging girl boner I have for him right now.

"What do you want to know?" Savini leans back in his chair, his resolve softening but his walls built up high. He isn't going to give me anything I don't pry out of him.

"Let's start with how old you are. That should be easy enough, right?"

"Forty-nine. You?"

"Twenty-eight."

"Does that satisfy your thirst for knowledge?"

"When's your birthday?" I ask him, unsure but hopeful he'll answer me.

"November 1st. Would you like my social security number, too?"

The waiter comes into the room again. "And for your second course, a sweet potato crisp with a goat cheese caviar." Somehow, he manages to replace our old plates with new ones in a fluid and swift motion.

"Thank you," I tell him as he leaves, and then focus on Savini. "Do you have a pen?"

"Why?" He straightens in his seat, coming closer to the table.

"For your social. That's a lot of numbers to memorize."

He ignores my request and pours another round of rye into the glass I hadn't realized I'd emptied. "Why law?"

"Why not?" My own walls fight to stay intact with such a simple, yet personal question. I chose law for many reasons, one being that I'm great at arguing with people and winning debates, but mainly because I wanted to be strong enough to protect those that needed protection. It was never about the money or accolades. No, it was something more. Something that haunts me to this day.

"You care about justice."

I pick up the sweet potato thing and look at him. "Don't you?"

"Believe it or not, I do."

His response is almost laughable, considering the dirt I already have on him. How can he possibly think that killing innocent people for hire is a noble or just career?

"And what is it you do for a living, Mr. Savini?"

"My job has many titles, really." He finishes his second course before continuing. "Enforcer...exterminator...pest control...handyman...you name it. If there's a situation that needs my attention, I take care of it."

"A...situation?" I bring my cup to my lips again and sip the sweet relief of the alcohol.

"Mmhm." He mocks me and does the same.

"We do have attorney-client privilege, Mr. Savini. You ensured that, when you spent fifty grand for two hours of my time. What you say in this room, stays in this room. It's my ethical duty to protect your confidentiality."

"How do I know you're not wearing a wire?"

"Suspicious much?" I stand from the table and motion to my body. "Check me."

"You're giving me permission to put my hands on you?"

"I'm giving you permission to verify I'm not wearing a wire." I swallow and wait for him to move.

His jaw tightens, and his fist clenches his napkin. Finally, he rises and comes over in front of me. Savini kneels before me, his large palms wrapping around my ankles and slowly inching their way higher, over my calf, the back of my knee.

I keep my sights trained forward, focusing all of my efforts on maintaining my breath.

Savini continues on his path, his hands swirling higher,

under my dress and over my thighs. "You're not wearing any panties." His fingers graze my hips but don't go any farther. Instead, he removes them and rises to his feet, returning his grasp to the outside of this expensive dress. His dark brown gaze forces my attention.

I stare up at him as he slides his hands over every inch of my body he can touch. My hands, my arms, my shoulders, the small of my back, all the way up to the sensitive skin on the nape of my neck, finishing with both of his hands wrapped around my cheeks, his fingers weaved through my hair.

If I didn't already want him badly, the lust I'm consumed in now…

Savini leans down, his nose resting against the top of my head. He breathes in, savoring me more than the twelve-course meal the chef has prepared us. "Fawn," he whispers.

The door to the kitchen swings open, pulling him out of his trance. He steps back, but I remain there, unable to gather myself. I suck in a long draw of air and steady the whirlwind of thoughts running through my head.

He is the enemy, Banks. Nothing more.

CHAPTER FIVE

Ourse after course. Drink after drink. We continue this
mindfuck of an evening.

We went back to small talk once he confirmed I wasn't
wearing a wire, but with more alcohol filling our systems, I
hope to uncover more of the truth than just his favorite color.

Which happens to be red.

He also enjoys classical music—the likes of Chopin and
Brahms, a bit of Bach. He claims it helps calm his raging nerves.
I wonder what would calm my raging hormones?

"Tell me about your family," Savini says when the waiter
takes our…I don't know, maybe fifth plate? They're all starting
to blur together at this point, and Savini told the waiter to stop
talking a few courses ago.

"Um…" I sip some water, a droplet of condensation falling
onto my lap.

"Start with your mother." He guides me like he knows it's
questionable territory.

I sigh, still studying that one single drop that landed and is
now fading away into nothing as it's absorbed into the chair

beneath me. Like all things, eventually they must come to an end.

"She was..." I look up at him. "Beautiful, really. Although, I don't think that's a fitting way to describe her." I bite at my lip and trail my gaze downward, recalling a memory. Countless come rushing in all at once, and without focusing on any specific vision, tears well in my eyes. "She had this radiance to her. She could captivate any audience."

When I don't continue, he speaks, "You talk about her in the past tense."

I nod, wiping at my cheek and reaching for my rye. "Yeah, she's dead." I continue before he can say the two words everyone else always says. "You don't have to say you're sorry. It was a long time ago."

"What happened?" His jaw tenses.

Maybe it's the fact that I plan on killing him. Or the numerous ounces of strong rye I've already drank, but my mouth opens, the truth spilling out. "My dad—or well—my stepdad, adoptive dad, whatever you want to call the piece of shit. He killed her."

I've only ever told Violet the real story of what happened to my mom. And only the bits and pieces I've been capable of sharing. Not the fact that the man who raised me took out his anger on not just my mom, but me and my half-brother Jared, too. He beat my mom to death one drunken night and threatened to kill Jared and me if we told the police the truth. He fed them a bullshit lie that she fell down the stairs, hit her head too hard, and bled out before help arrived. But Jared and I saw what he had done. I tried to pull him off of her, but he shoved me in a closet, locking me in there, only letting me out long enough to scare me into the story he wanted me to tell the cops. I didn't say a word. Not when the ambulance came. Not when the social workers showed up. Not when the few friends I had at school asked me where the bruises on my arms came from.

He stopped hitting me in places that would leave a visible mark. Only punching me in the ribs, anywhere on my torso, the back of my head. There was one day that Jared woke me up, shaking me profusely, his own eyes filled with tears. Blood was caked on my face; my nose was broken. Jared had thought I was dead and that he had been left alone with that vicious man.

No one ever questioned more than surface level what went on behind closed doors. No one investigated the death of my mother. No one came to save us from that monster.

Savini's gruff voice pulls me out of my tormented memories. "Was he ever brought to justice?"

"No."

"That's the thing about me and you, fawn. You went to school to do things your way, and I take things into my own hands."

I narrow my gaze at him. "What do you mean?"

"I bring justice to those like your supposed father."

"You kill bad guys?"

His stare bores into mine. "Yes."

But if that's the case, how does that explain Jared? He was a nobody college kid. I understand he worked for a criminal, but that doesn't mean he deserved to die. A slap on the wrist, maybe, but not death in an alley.

His death was a coverup, just like my mother's.

"I don't believe you," I tell him.

"Just last week, a man shoved his pregnant wife down the stairs when she accused him of cheating. She lived; the baby died."

"And him?"

"Fish food."

"You're not serious."

"There's this little strip club on the west side. Caters to working college girls. The owner has a recruiter he sends over to Marshall University on the regular." Savini shrugs. "None of that is a big deal. Those women make the decision to do that line of work, that's on them. But when the silent partner starts to get rough with the girls, threatening them out of nearly eighty percent of their earnings..." He looks at me. "I'm not going to tell you the rest of what he's done, but I can tell you, it will never happen ever again."

Is what he's saying really true?

"There were these two guys who worked for my main employer. Punk-ass little kids. Nearly a dozen assault charges against them they paid to have go away. Countless girls they attacked without an ounce of remorse. Entitled brats. I left them to bleed out and rot in an alley."

My heart skips a beat. Did he...no...that can't possibly be... Jared would never, not after what his father did to us—to our mother?

Tears roll down my cheeks without a care in the world that I don't want them to be there.

"I'm sorry, I didn't mean to upset you." Savini reaches across the table and latches onto my hand.

I pull it away from him and stand. "I have to get out of here. I can't do this." I latch onto my clutch and storm out of the secluded room we've been playing pretend in. I march my way through the restaurant, furiously wiping at my face. Why can't I stop crying?

My expensive heels click loudly against the polished floor of the lobby.

A doorman opens the door as I approach, and I burst out onto the sidewalk, blinking at my surroundings. The ground glistens with what must have been an evening rainfall. With not a car in sight, I reach into my bag and pull out my phone, poking and swiping and desperately wishing for a nearby ride-share.

There's a three-hour wait on one. Four on another. I click the first, but then it flashes unavailable.

"What the fuck!" I yell out.

Savini rushes out onto the sidewalk with me. "Banks, I'm sorry."

"Stop fucking saying that." I shove my phone in his face. "Why are there no fucking cars available? Where the hell are we? Fucking Narnia?"

"Calm down." He shoves his hand into his pocket and pulls out his own cell.

"Don't tell me to *calm down*."

"I'll have my driver take you home."

I shake my head. "No absolutely fucking not." Rule number whatever the fuck: don't let them find out where you live. It's bad enough that he knows my name, where I work, and my fucking childhood trauma. Not all of it, but enough that I can never take back.

"Okay." He lowers his phone. "What can I do then? What will make things better?"

I rake my hands through my hair, turning and realizing I'm standing in front of a hotel. Duh. I'll get a room. Hide away in a comfy robe until dawn, and then catch a ride when they're available. I'll fucking hitchhike if I have to.

"You don't have to fix anything, Savini. You've done enough." I march back to the door, the thing opening wide with my approach. I say a borderline aggressive, "Thank you," to the man no doubt wondering what the fuck is wrong with me and head straight to the front desk. "I'd like a room, please. Anything, I don't care what it is."

The straight-faced, tall man clicks away on his computer. "I'm afraid we have no available reservations for this evening."

With my debit card in hand, I stare blankly at him. "That can't be possible. Can you check again? Please? Put me in a broom closet for all I care."

Footsteps approach from the same direction I just came.

Still looking at the clerk, I say, "There's a big, scary, yet incredibly attractive man standing behind me isn't there?"

His gaze flits to Savini and then to me. He nods. "Mmhm."

"Banks," Savini calls out with a strange sort of tenderness to his voice.

I turn on my heel. "Yes?"

"I have a penthouse upstairs." He holds his hands up in front of him. "Not expecting anything, and surely you know by now what kind of person I am."

Do I though? Do I really?

At the end of the day, he's still a murderer.

But does that change because he claims to only kill bad guys?

There's no way Jared would do the things he said. His friend maybe, but not him. Not when his mother was a victim. His sister. Him. How could someone ever do what our father did to us, to another person?

Lying, cheating, deceit—those are one thing, but physical abuse? No. Never to someone who didn't deserve it. Like what I had thought of Savini. I was going to kill him because he murdered my brother. But what kind of person would that make me if what he was saying was true? That my brother was just as guilty as the man who took my mother from me.

Tears roll down my cheeks again. "I don't know why I'm crying so much."

Savini sighs and steps forward. He looks to the clerk. "I'll take it from here, Donno." Savini places his large hand on my shoulder and guides me away from the front desk and over to an elevator that's only accessible by keycard.

A few moments later, we step into his room, the aroma of cedar and honeysuckle tickling my nose. He continues to nudge me along until I'm sitting on a plush couch in the lavish sitting area in the middle of the place. Savini latches onto the box of tissues on the side table and extends them out to me. "I shouldn't have pushed you into talking about something you clearly didn't want to. I understand what it's like to bury things in the past."

I blow my nose, not caring about how incredibly unattractive it must be. "You know what sucks?"

"Hmm?" Savini puts his hands on his lap.

"It's not that I don't *want* to talk about her. Of course, I do. She was my favorite person. But it's like, all these good memories are overpowered by the bad ones. What he did to her. What he did to us." I sigh and close my eyes. "I'll never forget that, and no matter how hard I try to think of the good, I'm always overcome by the bad." I open up to find him still in the same position, like he's afraid I'm a bomb ready to explode, and he doesn't want to make any sudden moves. How funny, considering he's the killer I wish I could be.

"Can I tell you a secret?" Savini picks at his thumb with his index finger.

I chuckle and look at the time on my phone. "I'd say you were still within your two hours, but it's been almost four."

Savini reaches into his pocket to pull out a money clip. He slides the stack of cash out from under the fancy silver and puts it in my hand. "This should buy me a little more time, right?"

I push the money back toward him. "This one's on the house." I hold out my pinkie. "Pinkie promise."

Savini side-eyes me. "You're serious?"

"Yep. The ultimate promise. Unbreakable. More iron-clad than any contract I've ever written up." I nudge him with my elbow. "And I'm kind of a big deal."

He wraps his pinkie around mine and our hands stay together as they rest at our sides.

"I, uh…"

I sniffle and wait for him to find the words.

"I lost my mom when I was young, too. Similar story, really. So, while I'm not saying I understand what you've been through, because no one other than you shares that pain, I do have an idea."

"Are we trauma bonding right now?" I squeeze his hand and offer him a soft smile despite my snot nose and flushed face.

"I guess so." Savini leans onto the couch and puts his arm over the back. "And before we even had dessert."

I frown dramatically. "Not dessert."

He moves the hair out of my tear-streaked face. "Why don't you change out of those stuffy clothes, and I'll have it brought up?"

I tilt my head at him. "I thought you were being a gentleman, and here you are, trying to get me naked."

"Don't mistake my occasional kindness for being a gentleman, I'm nothing of the sort. I literally kill people for a living, and I thoroughly enjoy it." He rises to his feet. "And that warning I'm sure Axel gave you, you should have probably listened to him." Savini points to a closed double door leading to another room. "Bathroom is through there. You can borrow something of mine to wear to bed."

I follow his directions, going into the room and closing the door behind me. I rummage in a few of the drawers until I find a white tee shirt that will no doubt fall to my knees. I take it into the bathroom with me, and slide out of the overpriced heels and dress, throwing the thing over my head and breathing in the cinnamon smell of him that remains even after being cleaned. I finger through the little bottles on the counter and settle on one that says face wash. I make myself at home, despite being in the enemy's quarters, an idea that seems so foolish at this point.

Can he still be the enemy even after what I know now?

Savini made a few accusations but that doesn't mean they're true. And what if he wasn't even talking about Jared at all? I have to do some investigating before I fully believe that my abused half-brother turned into an abuser himself.

Feeling better than when I stepped into this penthouse, I

walk barefoot out of the bathroom, and bedroom, to find Savini closing the front door. A cart with a few metal trays sits near the entrance, and he pushes it over to the couch.

"I wasn't sure what you liked so I got..." He looks up at me and stops in the middle of his sentence. "Everything."

I sit on the couch, pulling a throw pillow on my lap to hide the fact that I'm not wearing anything under his tee. I could have probably found some oversized sweatpants, but my mind wasn't operating at peak performance five minutes ago. Not that it is now, either, as I study this seductive older man move from one end of the room to the other.

Is it the lingering alcohol in my veins? The sight of his rugged yet gorgeous exterior? Knowing that he punishes bad guys for a living? Or maybe the rich maple scent of him wafting by? Whatever it is, I'd rather him serve me up for dessert instead.

"Cheesecake, tiramisu, chocolate cake, French apple cake, blackberry mousse tart, crème brûlée." He uncovers another tray. "And an assortment of macaroons."

"What if I told you I don't care for any of those?"

He turns toward me, his gaze scanning my features. "Then I'd say you were a liar. And force feed you all of them."

"You wouldn't." I smack him playfully with the pillow on my lap.

Savini latches onto it and tosses it aside, sitting incredibly close to me, his right hand resting on my bare knee, his left reaching for something from our massive dessert spread. A second later, he's holding a forkful of the chocolate cake. "Open up."

Without meaning to, I inch my knees apart, quickly pushing them back together and opening my mouth, the thing he intended for me to spread wide for him. Not my damn legs.

He slides the fork carefully into my mouth, his gaze trained on mine as he slowly pulls it out. "Do you like that?"

I nod, like the obedient little thing I am, which is so fucking unlike me. This man, the enemy, has me practically eating out of the palm of his hand and enjoying it.

"Your turn." I lean forward, stealing the fork from his grasp and getting him a bite of the decadent cake. For a brief moment, I think he's not going to comply, but he parts his lips and allows me to enter him with the dessert.

I don't ignore his seductive gaze, the intimacy of us having the same utensil in our mouths, being this close to him with next to nothing on. I lick the rest of the cake off the fork, my eyes glued on him the whole time.

This is a dangerous game we're playing.

"What's next?" I ask him, fully prepared to go along with whatever he's about to say.

But, like something snaps him out of his trance, he snags the fork from me. "Try this cheesecake."

And with that, the tension is reeled in from his end, snuffing out my flame and reminding me why I'm here. To gather intel, not fuck the man who killed my brother. Because regardless of the reason, he's still his murderer.

We make our way through the fine selection of treats—the chocolate cake definitely my favorite of them all. Maybe because I'm a sucker for something rich and sinful, maybe because of the brief intimacy we shared.

I cover my mouth as a yawn escapes me. "I'm beat." My eyes close, my head leans into the cushy couch, and the next thing I'm aware of, Savini is carrying me.

"Shh, fawn." He tucks me into the bed and it's then that I notice he's wearing a tee shirt and grey sweatpants.

I sit upright and rub my face. "There's only one bed, where are you going to sleep?"

Savini nods at the other pillow. "A gentleman would sleep on the couch, but I told you I wasn't one."

My heart races faster, a million thoughts running through my mind.

"I put your phone on the charger and your purse on the table." He nods behind me, and when I turn, I spot both of them sitting there on my side of the bed. "Get some sleep, fawn." He climbs in next to me while keeping his distance and pushes a button on a remote to turn the lights off.

The pitch-black darkness seems to soothe my nerves. I lie back onto my pillow and reach for my clutch, just to confirm it's still there and didn't disappear in the last five seconds.

I listen to the steady rhythm of his breaths, my own chest rising and falling in time with his. I stare into the depths of nothing, each blink waking me up more and more. I fell asleep easily on the couch, but now, next to him, in the same bed, rest will no doubt evade me.

I reposition myself, accidentally bumping into him in the process. "Sorry," I mutter.

But instead of responding verbally, he skims his finger along the side of my arm.

A chill floats over me, and I revel in the momentary bliss of his touch. I swallow, contemplating how I should react. I lean into his caress. Is it a mistake? Probably, but my vagina doesn't care.

He grips my forearm, and that signal is enough to send me climbing on top of him, only he doesn't expect the knife I put to his throat, the one I latched onto when I was confirming my bag was still there.

With my body straddling his, and the blade at his throat, I can almost hear the smile on his face. "Are you trying to turn me on, fawn?"

I push the thing harder, no doubt drawing a bit of blood. "Were you telling me the truth? About what you do?" I have to get to the bottom of what happened to my brother.

"I hurt people, it's what I do. Good or bad, it doesn't matter."

He pauses and adds, "I kill people who deserve it." Savini's erection grows beneath me, pressing through his sweatpants onto my bare bottom.

I settle some of the weight of my body down on him and nearly moan at the pressure.

Savini continues, "I can feel your wetness through my bottoms, fawn. So this must be turning you on, too." He sits up, disregarding the blade that slices against his throat with the motion. If the lights were on, there would surely be a trail of his blood. He grips my waist, pulling me closer. "Do you want me?"

Do I want to kill him or fuck him? The answer is still yes to both.

But I can only get one of those things right now. And the greedy part of me chooses the latter.

"Do you have a condom?" I say, my breath catching.

He fumbles with the nightstand, pulling out a drawer and grabbing what I can only assume is a rubber. "You have to tell me you want this, fawn."

"I'm soaked, isn't it obvious?" I weave my hand through his hair, the other still holding onto the knife.

His voice deepens. "Tell me."

"I want you, please, God damn it. Fuck me right now, Lorenzo." I grind against his shaft and wish there was no fabric separating us.

"You've never called me by my first name." He rips the package open, shoves his pants down, and secures the condom. Savini reaches down, his hand finding my slit. "You're so wet, fawn." He teases my entrance, and I do everything I can to guide myself onto his fingers, his cock, anything to penetrate and save me from this torment.

I bring the knife back to his throat. "Fuck me."

Savini chuckles and I wish like hell I could see the smile on his face. "As you command." In one solid motion, he wraps his arm around my waist and flips me onto my back, his body towering over mine. He readies his cock at my hole, his thumb skimming my clit. Without restraint, he shoves himself inside of me, filling and spreading me in ways that have me screaming out. "Is that what you want, fawn? You want me to ruin you?" He snatches the knife from me, pins my hands over my head, and places the blade at my throat all while thrusting into me with force. "You want it rough? Is that it?"

"Y-yes," I tell him, having no idea myself that that's what I desired. But now that he's giving it to me, I can't help but want more. More deepness. More pain. More of him.

I've had rough sex before, but nothing of this magnitude. Never with a man this old. And certainly not with a sharp blade cutting into my flesh.

Savini leans down, breathing me in. "Your pussy is so tight around my cock, fawn. I could stay inside you all night."

I push forward, against the knife, and find his lips with mine. I swirl my tongue over his and bite his bottom lip, dragging it into my mouth. "I can't last all night."

"I know." Savini rocks his hips, putting more pressure on my clit with each thrust.

"Fuck," I moan, my climax shattering me around him. A wave of pleasure floods me from head to toe, and I ride it like there's no tomorrow.

"That's my girl." Savini thrusts harder and kisses me deeper. "I want you to come for me again, fawn. Can you do that for me?"

I mumble something, my brain at a loss for forming any kind of intelligible response. Another orgasm? After the one I just had? Impossible.

But the second he puts the knife to my throat, my desire heightens, that tightness in my core rising once again.

"You like that? You like when I fuck you hard? When I hurt you?"

"Mmm." The scent of blood lingers. The pain from the cut enhances my pleasure. "Come with me, please," I beg him.

Only, I can't wait for him any longer. My climax comes without my permission.

Savini grunts and fucks me with no limitation, his body knocking into mine with a force so strong I'm sure I'll be walking with a limp tomorrow. If I can walk at all. And I take every bit of it, grateful for the satisfaction.

He slows his pace until he stops completely, his forehead resting on mine. He breathes, "Did I hurt you?"

"Yes," I tell him.

"Are you okay?"

"Yes."

Savini climbs off of me and a moment later, a dim light fills the room. "I shouldn't have been so rough."

I sit up, scooting over to him and resting my head on his shoulder. "I'm the one who brought a knife to bed."

He takes in a breath and sighs. "Let's get you cleaned up." Savini reaches for my hand, tugs me over, pulls me into his arms, and carries me to the bathroom, where he turns on another low light. He gently sets me on the counter and opens the cupboards until he finds what he's looking for.

Meticulously, he cleans the few wounds on my neck and puts a giant, gaudy bandage over them.

I meet his gaze as he works. "This was one-hundred-percent consensual; I promise."

His jaw tenses but he doesn't respond.

"Let me." I tend to the damage I did to him, trying to pay him as much attention as he did me, and when I'm done, I hop off the counter and relieve myself. No need for a UTI along with the flesh wounds.

I come out to find that he's changed and is putting a new set of sheets on the bed. He gives me another shirt, since the one I'm wearing has a mixture of our blood speckled all over it, and a pair of his sweat shorts to put on. I draw the strings tight around my waist to prevent them from immediately falling off.

It isn't long until his breaths even out, lulling him fast to sleep. I doze in and out, but wake with the sun, sneaking out of his penthouse before he can notice I'm no longer by his side.

I don't regret sleeping with the enemy, it's just now, I have no idea how to move forward.

CHAPTER SIX

I dig through my notes and try to find a connection, any thread that can point me in the right direction on how to uncover the truth.

The terrible reality that my dead brother wasn't a victim after all.

I had been so focused on the who, that I never quite figured out the why. I didn't need to know. I had all the information I needed. Jared had been murdered, and I would avenge his death. I would bring justice to his killer since the system had failed him. It's not exactly why I went to school to be an attorney, but sometimes we have to take the law into our own hands if we want things done.

Had I acted irrationally, based purely on my revenge-fueled rage, I would have killed Savini without uncovering any of this. Now, I must cross my t's and dot my i's if I'm going to be confident in taking someone else's life. I should have never been this careless.

That stops today. I will piece this together if it's the last thing I do.

A knock at my door sends the papers falling out of my

hands. I glance at my phone and hope whoever it is will go away.

Only, they don't.

Another rumble, this time louder, more urgent.

I huff and stand, dusting off my jeans and stomping toward my interruption. "Can I help you?" I say while opening the door.

The thing bursts out of my hand and stone-faced as ever, Lorenzo Savini waltzes into my apartment.

How the fuck did he find out where I live? And why is he here?

I tuck my hair behind my ear and come up with the best thing I can think of. "I'm sorry I didn't say goodbye when I left. I had some important work to get done for a project…"

Savini holds his finger out in front of me. "I don't want to hear it."

I cross my arms and narrow my gaze. "Excuse me?"

He shoves past me, walking right over to the haphazard piles of papers.

"You can't—"

But he doesn't care about my protest.

He picks up one of the pages, looks it over and then tosses it aside. "Does Axel know about this?"

My heart thuds against my ribcage. "What?" How could he possibly have gathered what that was after studying it for two seconds?

Savini takes a long breath in and exhales. "Jared."

I do everything I can not to react, but my widened eyes are no doubt a dead giveaway.

"You weren't that hard to find, you know?" Savini slowly strolls around my living room, scanning the contents. "Banks Manor. You have your mother's last name. But a quick search shows you have a half-brother, who, naturally, took his father's last name."

He continues to wander around my apartment while I remain frozen in place.

"I should have known when you started asking questions." Savini shakes his head methodically and clicks his tongue. "I should have been more cautious when a random, stunning woman showed up at a known criminal gathering place, a lost little deer, wandering into a lion's den. I should have connected the dots when I saw you with Axel. But no..." He rubs his forehead. "I was too fucking blinded to see what was right in front of me."

Savini takes a few steps toward me. My entire body tenses.

"You don't know who you're fucking with, fawn." His stare is deadly. "You need to tell Axel, or I'm going to." He clenches his jaw. "You're lucky I don't kill you right here and now."

I swallow harshly. "Why don't you?"

He balls his hand into a fist. "Because I understand what it's like to want revenge. But what you don't get is that revenge is a poison that will seep into your soul, eating you alive from the inside. And the moment you act on it, you can never come back from that." Savini exhales and loosens his grip. "I don't want that for you. Save yourself before it's too late."

I say the thing I've wanted to say to him from the moment I set my sights on him. "You killed my brother."

"I did what had to be done. Your *brother* was not a good person, fawn."

"Stop fucking calling me that," I blurt out. "And stop lying. You're just trying to justify being a murderer."

"If you don't believe me, that's fine. Why don't you talk to one of his victims?"

I steady my raging heartbeat. Is he about to give me a lead? Or a false story only to validate his own?

"Claire Cooper, she goes by Jones now, but I hear she and Johnny are in town. They visit Bram's religiously. If you want the truth, go talk to her. But I warn you, that place is heavily trafficked by people you don't want to cross."

"How do I know you're not just feeding me a line of bullshit?"

Savini shrugs. "You don't, but it would be a lot easier just to kill you before you stick your nose in the wrong person's business. Consider this my parting gift to you."

The finality of his last statement slices through me without warning.

"Bram's…that's the diner near where Jared was killed?"

"Mmhm."

"And this Johnny, his name sounds familiar. Is he the same guy who was shot over there?"

Savini nods.

"I thought he was dead."

"You're not the only one." Savini stalks toward me, stopping only inches from my body. "What we had was fun." He skims his finger along the cut on my neck. "But you and I both know what happens when you throw gasoline on a fire." His gaze dips down to my lips before he walks away and pauses at my door. "Tell Axel." And then he's gone.

I stand there, in the silence and allow my mind to run rampant.

Claire. Johnny. Jared.

Savini knows the truth. Axel is caught in the crossfire.

I'm left with the burning question—can I trust Lorenzo Savini?

—◉—

I have the ride-share driver drop me off a couple blocks from my destination in hopes that the fresh air on the rest of my journey will help clear my head and come up with a game plan.

Savini said Claire visits Bram's religiously, but that doesn't mean she's there now. What will I even say to her if she is?

Hey, did my brother sexually assault you? Do you know of any of his other victims that would be willing to talk to me about their traumatic experience? What right do I even have to bring up something so terribly if these girls really are his victims?

Until I truly know, Jared will remain a victim in my mind. And if he really is an abuser, he doesn't deserve an ounce of my pity.

After everything he and I went through, there's no way he would treat someone the same way our father did. Unless...he became the man we hated. I would have known, would have seen the signs, wouldn't I? His own sister should have noticed the red flags if he was what Savini claims he is. But Jared and I outgrew our closeness once we got old enough to sneak out of the house and escape the torment of our dad. We went our separate ways, fleeing the abuse however we could. And once we became adults, that distance manifested even more. FaceTime calls to catch up morphed into texts left on read.

So, when I heard the news that he had been killed, it hit me like a freight train. Grief, guilt, anger—it filled me all at once. Had I been there, maybe I could have saved him. If I insisted that we stayed in touch more, maybe I could have prevented him from going down a path of crime that resulted in his death. I could have done more. I *should* have done more.

I open the door to the diner, the bell chiming on my way in. The scent of freshly baked goods hits me immediately.

I'm greeted by a grey-haired older man from behind the register. "Welcome in. Sit wherever you'd like." He goes back to work checking out the customer in front of him.

I slide into the first booth available and steady myself on the seat.

A waitress approaches—jet-black hair and a seriously wicked case of resting-bitch-face. The second she pulls out her notepad, she softens and transforms into the customer service version of herself. "What can I get you?"

"Coffee, black. Thank you." Nothing like some caffeine to really get these nerves kicking in high gear.

She doesn't bother writing my order down, or saying anything else. She just turns on her heel and marches back to the counter, where she grabs a mug and one of the few carafes of coffee.

The bell at the door rings again and catches her attention. She does a double take, and the second glance makes her face break out into a huge smile.

A man, covered in tattoos and looking like he belongs on a poster somewhere grabs her by the waist and kisses her.

She giggles and sneaks out of his grasp. "Magnus, I'm working." She nods toward the booth in the corner. "You're going to have to wait."

"Whatever you say, princess." Magnus complies and settles into the far end of the diner.

The girl comes over and sets the cup on my table. "Sorry about that, my boyfriend is rather impatient." She fills the thing with coffee.

Before she can walk away, I open my mouth. "Could I ask you a question?"

"Yeah, shoot." She glances behind her quickly. "The special is blueberry pancakes with a side of bacon."

I follow her gaze and then do my own double-take. Written on the board in white chalk is *The Claire Special*, with the food she just told me listed underneath.

"Who is that? Claire?"

The waitress nonchalantly says, "A girl that used to work here."

"Oh."

"Yeah, her husband and the owner go way back. They're pretty much family."

"Oh."

"So." She widens her eyes expectantly. "Would you like to order?"

I shake my head. "No, sorry, I just...I was just wondering who she was."

The bell chimes again.

Looking a bit annoyed, the waitress points her pen toward the door. "There she is if you want to ask her what her obsession with blueberry pancakes is."

I turn to witness a beautiful woman stroll into the diner, her cheeks aglow from the beaming smile on her face. She walks straight up to the older man who had greeted me and wraps her arms around his neck. "Bram!" She squeezes him.

"You made it," he says, hugging her back with just as much enthusiasm. "Where's Johnny?"

Claire walks behind the counter and pours herself a cup of coffee, taking the cinnamon shaker and sprinkling a few dashes inside. "He had a work thing to do, but he'll be here soon."

Magnus rises from his spot in the corner and approaches the bar area. "Hey, Claire-bear."

"Hey, Maggie."

Claire and Magnus share a fist bump.

She cranes her neck to look back to where he came from. "Where's Hayes and Dom?"

"Hayes is probably brooding somewhere, and Dom is at the meeting with Johnny."

"Oh, right, duh." Claire elbows the waitress. "How's June?" She blows on her coffee and takes a cautious sip.

"I'll be happier when I don't have a bodyguard with me twenty-four seven." June flits her gaze to the other end of the place where a guy who weirdly resembles Ian Somerhalder stands with his arms crossed.

"It's for your protection," Magnus tells her.

She rolls her eyes and grabs the plate that the cook shoves

through the open window area. June nods in my direction. "Customer over there was asking about The Claire Special. Why don't you go sell it to her yourself?"

I force my gaze down at my steaming cup of coffee and pretend I wasn't spying on their entire conversation.

"Afternoon," a gentle voice says.

"Hi," I manage to respond.

"I hear you were curious about the special so I wanted to come introduce myself." She extends her hand. "I'm Claire."

I place my hand in hers. "Banks."

"Oh, what a cool name. I don't think I've ever heard it before."

I nervously chuckle. "Yeah, I don't know what my mom was thinking, honestly. She was probably too high on drugs to think of anything else."

Claire smiles. "Moms." There's a strange undertone to the way she says it like there's so much more to the word than what she leads on.

But learning about her own childhood trauma isn't why I'm here, I came to learn the truth about Jared.

"Could I, um, ask you a question?"

Claire bobs her head up and down. "Of course."

I point to the seat across from me. "Would you mind sitting?" I reluctantly glance over at the menacing tattooed guy still sitting on a stool at the bar who's currently chatting with the owner.

Claire hesitates but decides to go along with my request. "Is everything okay?"

"Yeah, I..." I fiddle with the handle on my mug. "I don't know how to..."

Completely unexpectedly, Claire reaches forward and latches onto my hand. "I promise I don't bite. Don't let my name on a chalkboard fool you, I'm no one special."

Her kindness trickles into me and gives me the courage to

open my mouth. "Did you know the guys who were killed near here a while back?"

Claire freezes and then pulls her hand away.

"Did you know Jared?" Tears well in my eyes and it's everything I can do to hold them at bay.

She starts to speak, then stops, then starts again, only to stop again.

Magnus walks over, his frame towering over us, casting a shadow on the table. Jesus, he's even more gorgeous and intimidating up close. "Everything okay over here?"

Claire forces a smile. "Yeah, Maggie, we're good."

His stare burns a hole through the side of my head but he accepts her statement and goes over to his corner booth.

She lowers her voice. "Are you a cop?"

I furiously shake my head. "No, oh God no." I can only imagine how stupid it would be for a cop to walk in here asking questions after the warning Savini gave me and seeing the muscle already in this place. If I weren't an unsuspecting female, Magnus and the Ian lookalike would have been enough to scare me out of here already.

But if I've learned anything from my time on this planet, being a woman can get you access to places you typically wouldn't be allowed.

"I knew him." Claire's nostrils flare and she repositions herself.

"Claire, listen, I'm going to share something with you that I don't like to talk about, but I think it might help you better understand why I'm here..."

Claire inches closer like she's aware whatever this is I'm about to say is private information.

"I lost my mom when I was younger." I note her resolve softening. I sigh and continue, digging my fingers into my thigh to steady myself for this admission. I've gone years without talking about this and here I am, spilling the tea back-to-back to practically strangers. "My adopted father, he beat her to death, while my brother and I watched." I shake my head as if I can get rid of the memory or make it any less true. "He was a monster, and his rage didn't stop there. He was never caught, never penalized for taking her life, or what he did to us. We didn't get free of him until we were old enough, but the damage had already been done."

"Banks, I'm..." But she stops herself as if realizing her apology isn't going to change what happened.

"I *need* to know, Claire. The truth about Jared, what kind of person he was." I lean forward. "I know about the cover-up, okay? I don't need any more lies."

Claire seems to process the information, her face a bit unreadable and only adding to my continued frustration. Finally, a million seconds later, she responds. "Jared, he was your brother."

I can't tell whether it's a question or that she's acknowledging what we both already know.

I nod, a single tear rolling down my cheek.

Claire chews at her lip. "I don't want to taint this idea you have of him."

"And I don't want to mourn a version of a man that never existed." I fight with how much more I'm willing to share, but decide to go on anyway. "I tracked down his killer, Claire. I wanted vengeance. I couldn't go through it again, a death at someone's hand that wasn't deserved. But I need to know if what I'm fighting for is worth it."

Claire's blue eyes widen. "He sent you to me?"

"Yes."

"Wow." She glances down then back up. "I'm surprised he didn't kill you himself..."

My phone vibrates with Axel's name at the top of the screen. I click the ignore button and focus on the girl holding all the cards in front of me.

"This fight, this war you're waging inside." Claire reaches across to me again. "And the one you're risking out here, with these *people*." She flits her gaze toward June's bodyguard in the corner. "I urge you to reconsider. It won't bring your brother back, and even if it did, you wouldn't like the man he became."

She confirms what Savini has been saying all along. Jared was a bad guy. And Savini killed him because of it. He rid the world of one more abuser—how could I ever punish him for that?

A weight seems to lift from my shoulders, but is immediately replaced by another.

This whole time I've been playing Axel to try to get close to Savini, I've dug myself into a hole I might not be able to get out from. Savini gave me a final warning and made it clear that if I continued to interfere, he would kill me, and if I didn't come clean with Axel, he would tell him himself. How can I diffuse a bomb that's already lit and ready to detonate?

CHAPTER SEVEN

Ihug Claire after we exchange numbers, and she assures me that June really isn't as mean as she appears to be.

"You think she and Magnus are intimidating, wait until you meet her other two boyfriends."

"Two?" I raise a brow at her.

She nods with a grin. "One man was never going to be enough for her. Heck, I'm not all that confident three is either."

I point to the Ian Somerhalder look-alike. "He isn't one of them?"

"Nope, Simon isn't, not that I'm aware, at least. Pretty sure the three she has would murder him if he tried."

"Interesting." I love a girl that's confident in what she wants and can take it. "Just Johnny for you?"

Claire holds her hand over her heart. "He's more than I ever could have asked for."

I wonder what it's like, to be *that* in love. Just the shift in her tone when she talks about him is enough to show how much he means to her. And after what I heard they went through, I can only imagine how strong their connection is.

"I'm happy for you," I tell her, because it's the truth. It doesn't take more than five minutes with Claire to see what kind of person she is.

She's pure, genuine, kind.

She didn't have to sit there and hear me out while I questioned her, and yet she did anyway, because she could tell I needed her in that moment. And here she is, making sure we stay in touch and bringing me into her friend group.

I hate that it brought our shared trauma to bring us together, but luckily there's one silver lining to this whole situation.

"Listen, I have to go, but I want to thank you for this. Really. I'm sorry for rehashing the past." I squeeze her forearm one last time.

"Don't worry about me," Claire tells me. "And hey, you're going to make it through this."

As much as I want to believe that I will, I'm not so sure. No matter how this plays out, I'm going to lose Axel *and* Savini. And then there's the wildcard of if I lose my life.

I walk out of the diner and slam into a hard body.

"Fuck," I blurt out.

Hands clasp my shoulders, steadying me. Wild eyes stare into mine. "Banks."

Axel pulls me into his arms, holding me so damn tight I can barely breathe.

I mumble into his chest and savor the warmth of his embrace.

"I was so fucking worried about you when you kept ignoring my calls." Axel lets go but keeps me at an arm's length to study me over. Through gritted teeth, he says, "Did he fucking do that?"

I touch the cuts on my neck. "It's fine. I'm fine." I blink up at him. "How did you know I was here?"

"When you didn't answer, I got freaked out and had my buddy trace your phone." He shakes his head. "Never mind that, what are you doing here? Are you crazy?" Axel glances behind me and into Bram's diner. "Come on." He weaves his hand through mine and tugs me away from the entrance.

Only, he doesn't realize that he leads me exactly to where my brother was killed.

I tense up and let go of him, not stepping any further into the alley.

"Talk to me, tell me what's going on." Axel turns around to face me.

This is it, the moment where I spill everything and lose him. When he finds out the truth, will he kill me and leave me for dead in this alley the same way Jared died? Is he a murderer like Savini? Or just an errand boy like Jared was?

"I…" If I say nothing, I lose him, if I tell him what I've done, I'll lose him, too. There's no potential outcome where both of us don't get hurt.

"Whatever it is, you don't need to be afraid of me, Banks." Axel tilts my face up at him. "I'm not the one who you should fear."

A chill runs up my spine.

"Savini will kill you. I don't know what you did to provoke him, but he's on a rampage today. You need to leave town, lay low for a little while until things blow over." Axel wipes a tear that rolls down my cheek. "I'll protect you, I will. But you need to tell me what happened."

I shake my head. "You won't if I do."

Axel grabs my hand and puts my pinkie in his. "I fucking promise. I'm not going to let him hurt you. No matter what."

I stare down at our interlocked fingers and slowly rock my head back and forth. "I'm not going to hold you to it."

"Just tell me, please, you're fucking killing me." Axel runs his palm over his tattooed neck.

"That double homicide that was in this alley," I tell him.

He glances behind his shoulder and back at me, his brows pinched together. "Yeah?"

"It was Savini."

Confusion still wrecks his face. "Okay..."

"One of the college kids he killed." I chew on the inside of my lip, afraid of losing him forever. I've broken so many of my own rules. "Was my brother."

His expression turns from pinched brows to wide-eyed. "Banks, oh my god. Come here." Axel drags me to him. "I'm so sorry."

I push him away. "That's not the worst of it."

He unwillingly allows the distance.

"I...I inserted myself into your life to get closer to him. I wanted revenge, I wanted to kill him for what he did. I was *so* mad." I choke back the sob that threatens to take hold. "I didn't mean to hurt you."

Axel stands there, his body not moving but his gaze flitting to each of my eyes. "This wasn't...this wasn't real?" He looks down and then at me again. "Any of it? This was all a lie?"

I wipe my nose. "In the beginning, but..."

He cuts me off. "Christ, Banks." Axel clutches his chest. "I...I loved you."

The past tense version of that word rips my heart into pieces. I've heard it before from other men but I never *wanted* to hear it until now. "Axel, I..."

He stops me again, holding his finger out to silence me, his beautiful eyes glistening. "I wasn't joking when I said he'd kill you, and I think you're well aware of what he's capable of." Axel rubs his lips together and checks his watch. "He's over on Marston's for probably another hour or two. You should use that time to get somewhere safe, somewhere he won't be able to find you." He skims the outline of one of the cuts on my neck. "Next time this will be much worse."

He leaves me in the alley, alone and struggling to figure out if the pain in my soul is from his absence or being this near where my brother died.

Either way, I can't stay here. Not in this dirty backstreet where I'm haunted by my past and present.

I knew I would lose him, but I never imagined the severity of what that would feel like. I went into this with rules, the same guidelines I've been living by for all of my adult life. I wasn't supposed to catch feelings. Not for him, not for Savini. They were pawns in this grand game of chess, and with them off the board, I'm left vulnerable and at risk of checkmate.

If I stand to salvage any of this, there's only one move left to make.

CHAPTER EIGHT

I wouldn't say Lorenzo Savini is predictable, but he is a creature of habit.

On a sheet of paper tucked lazily in a stack in my living room is a list of places he frequents. A hole-in-the-wall diner over on Marston's is one of them.

He's never consistently visited the place, making it difficult to narrow down when would be the most opportune time to confront him, but with Axel's warning, he gave me the information I needed.

I reposition my shirt and stroll through the front door, ignoring the pounding in my chest and wild stares that my arrival commands.

Men of all varieties look my way, which isn't ideal considering what I came here to do.

But if I've learned anything, people get away with murder all the time.

A tall, lanky twenty-something-year-old guy stands in front of me. "Can I help you with something?"

I shift my focus around the room. "Savini, where is he?"

"Not here." The guy broadens his shoulders to appear wider

and inches closer. He's sorely mistaken if he thinks that will intimidate me.

Mild chatter sounds from behind a door and I nod to it. "He's in there, isn't he?"

The man steps forward, his frame bumping into mine.

"Don't fucking touch me." I shove him with all my might, barely moving him.

Some of the guys laugh, and a couple of them stand up.

I ready myself to fist-fight this little bitch who thinks he can fuck with a girl. His pathetic attempt at masculinity is no match for my short-person syndrome.

Do I think I can win this battle? No.

But am I going to try? Fuck yeah.

"Who do you think you are? Coming in here like that?" The guy pushes me, sending me stumbling a few feet. "You fucking cunt." His hand forms a fist, and his arm winds back.

A shot rings out so loud my ears ring. The man's eyes widen and he lowers his gaze to his chest. Blood seeps through his shirt, slow at first and then pools all around the wound. His legs give out under him and he drops to his knees.

Behind him, Savini stands, his arm outstretched and a smoking gun in his grasp.

"Out, everyone fucking out," he commands of the room.

Without hesitating, all the people rush out the front door, scattering like their lives depend on it, because, well, they do.

When the place is empty, aside from the two of us and the newly dead man, Savini spits out, "What are you doing here?" He turns, going back into the room he was just in.

It's now or never, Banks. You came here for a reason, get on with it.

I follow him in, watching as he lowers his weapon onto the table and grabs the glass of golden liquid. He swallows it down and discards the cup carelessly. It bobbles before settling upright, almost falling off the edge.

"I asked you a question." His voice grows deeper. "What. Are. You. Doing. Here?" When I don't answer, he continues. "Give me one reason I shouldn't kill you."

I reach into my waistband, and pull out the gun I stole from Axel's apartment a week ago. I train it on him, my hands shaky but my aim steady. "Give me one reason I shouldn't kill *you*."

Savini turns, slowly, an unreadable expression on his face. He chuckles and steps closer. "Pull the trigger, fawn."

I grip the handle tighter, my finger itching to end this right here and now. But a mysterious force prevents me from following through with my plan.

"You killed my brother." Tears well in my eyes.

"We already went over this. He wasn't a good guy."

"Neither are you. You hurt people for a living."

"I get paid for what I'm good at."

"And what about me?"

"What about you?"

"Was hurting me just pro-bono? I told Axel the truth."

"You." Savini moves toward me, his eyes narrowing. "Did this to yourself." He continues until his chest is pressed against the barrel of my gun. "You're going to regret not pulling that trigger when you had the chance, Banks."

I'm struck by the memory of my knife at his throat, the way he pushed through it, and turned it on me, fucking me with force and making me climax harder than I ever have before. My gaze flicks down to the cut on his neck, similar to the one on mine. I recall him being afraid that he had hurt me and tending to the wounds with such care. He was rough, but then gentle.

In my momentary distractive state, he disarms me, pulls me to him, and shoves the gun into my ribcage. "You're fucking with the wrong type of people, fawn. I could end your life with a simple movement."

"Do it." I lean into the thing and wish he would shut up and put me out of my misery already.

I've lost my brother, twice now—first with his death, and then with the knowledge of the truth. I've lost Axel, I've lost Savini. My mother. Anyone I've ever truly cared for is gone.

I've made all these damn rules and did everything I could to block out my feelings but none of it protected me from being hurt.

Savini tightens his hold on my waist. "I once said you were like a butterfly—that this world would pluck your wings until there was nothing left of you. But I was wrong." He slowly guides the gun around my front. "You don't have the wings of a butterfly, you have the wings of a devil." He runs the barrel down until the chamber rubs between my legs.

I don't mean to, but I fucking moan.

"God damn." Savini grins and presses it harder against me. "You really are crazy."

Without giving it another thought, I stand taller and press my mouth on his. If I'm going to die today, at least it will be with one last orgasm.

Priorities, am I right?

Savini hesitates for a moment before kissing me back. "What are you doing?" he mutters.

I reach for his pants and unbutton them. "Just go with it."

His kiss deepens and he digs his fingers further into my side.

"I want you to fuck me." I shove my hand into his boxers and grip his already-growing erection.

"Are you sure?" Savini rests his forehead on mine. "And not just because I'm holding you at gunpoint."

"Yes."

"Bend over that desk." He nods toward the mahogany thing in the middle of the room.

I comply, walking around the front of it and leaning down on my elbows to face him. "What are you waiting for? Either shoot me or fuck me."

He shakes his head and follows me over, the gun still in his hand as he yanks my leggings over my ass and drags them to my ankles. Savini kneels behind me, one palm trailing up my leg and the other dragging the cold metal along my skin.

Impatiently, I arch back toward him and spread wider for him.

His fingers and the side of the gun continue toward my ass, both of them inching closer to my soaked entrance.

My mind runs wild at the possibilities of what's going to happen next while my heart pounds even crazier. Desire overcomes me, swirling me in a lust-filled frenzy I'm not sure I'll ever make it out of. I want—no, I need—this fucking release.

"You've been a bad girl, fawn." Savini teases me with the barrel, skimming it along the inside of my thigh. He blows on my pussy, and I tense at the minimal touch.

"Then punish me," I practically beg him.

"You'd like that, wouldn't you?" He brings the gun even closer, resting it against my hole.

Is he going to fuck me with the gun I brought here to kill him? And why am I so fucking turned on by that?

I push back on it, the thing barely penetrating me. "Oh God," I moan.

Savini removes it and stands. "If you're going to be screaming out anyone's name, it's going to be mine, fawn. Do you fucking hear me?" He fumbles in the drawer next to him, the sound of a condom wrapper following and him rubbing his sheathed cock over my entrance. "I said, do you hear me?"

"Y-yes."

"Let me hear you say it then."

"Lorenzo," I breathe, rocking my hips onto him, desperate for penetration.

"Good girl, fawn." He shoves his cock inside, slamming me forward.

My face presses against the hard surface and I reach to grip the edge of the desk to brace myself.

Savini slides his hand up my back, grabs a fistful of my hair, and ruthlessly fucks me. He keeps the gun on me at all times, and my sick fucking desire loves every second of it.

My core tightens and my climax inches closer and closer. I beg to hold it off but my senses are overloaded with pleasure.

The door to the front shop swings open and Savini immediately stops, his cock still buried in me as he removes the gun from me and points it at the intruder.

I blink to clear my vision of the stars and focus my sights on that beautiful, tattooed man I betrayed.

Axel has a pistol in his own grasp, holding it in front of him and training it on Savini. "Get off of her, you sick fuck."

Savini dares to slowly pump inside me while Axel threatens his life.

How can I possibly explain this to Axel when we left things the way we did?

He knows Savini wants to kill me, and here he is, fucking my brains out while holding me at gunpoint. I can only imagine what this must look like to Axel. But the truth might be worse than what he already thinks.

"I—" I struggle to gain my voice. "I can explain."

"Explain?" Axel inches closer.

Savini pushes into me again. "I'm going to shoot your boyfriend and keep fucking you if you don't hurry, fawn."

"As bad as this seems, it's…" I try to sit up a little to face him. "Consensual."

Axel's blue eyes grow wider. "What?"

"And if you don't mind, we were in the middle of something," Savini tells him.

"You're not going to kill her?" Axel continues toward us. Dangerously close to Savini's poised gun.

"Does it look like it?" Savini rocks in and out of me.

"I knew you'd do something stupid." Axel meets my gaze.

"But this isn't what I expected." His arms relax slightly, not so eager to blast off a shot at Savini.

Savini sighs. "Either shut up, join us, or get the fuck out."

I swallow harshly and wait for Axel's response.

Axel creeps into the room fully, walking all the way over to me, his gun lazily pointed at the man fucking me from behind. He smooths the hair out of my face. "I wasn't lying when I said you were pretty."

"Yeah?" My heart swells, along with my ever-hungry want for him.

"I shouldn't have left you." Axel skims his finger over my cheek, completely ignoring the fact that I'm still being railed.

I reach for him, tugging at his waistband and pulling him closer. "I'm sorry, Axel."

It's his move now—the ball is in his court.

He skims his thumb over my bottom lip, unzips his pants, and pulls out his cock. "Show me what that pretty mouth can do."

I grin and lick my lips, pressing my tongue to my bottom teeth and plunging him into another one of my ravenous holes.

Savini's cock throbs inside of me and he picks up his pace, lowering his gun to rest on my right shoulder.

Axel moans and rocks his hips, fucking my mouth and putting his own weapon on my other side.

Two guns. Two cocks. One girl.

Match made in fucking heaven.

I grumble against Axel's cock and take every inch of Savini that he gives me. My eyes water but this time not from sadness. I grip the base of Axel's shaft and pump him into my mouth, welcoming the lack of restraint either of these men gives me.

My climax approaches again, this time giving me almost no warning as it floods over me. I clench my pussy around Savini which only makes him fuck me harder. It shoves me into Axel, who takes the courtesy of pulling my hair to the side as he face fucks me.

They fuck me all the way through my orgasm and keep ravishing me until another one builds. This time, Savini bundles my hair into his hand, freeing Axel to pull his own cock out while he jerks it onto my face. He finishes while Savini forcefully blows his load into my pussy. Their own pleasure fuels mine as I pulsate around Savini's throbbing cock once again.

I scream out and lick my lips, so fucking satisfied but somehow still wanting more.

Savini pulls out of me, stripping himself of the condom and tossing it into the wastebasket next to his desk. He kneels, takes a long lick of my freshly fucked pussy, and pulls his pants up.

Axel leans down and kisses my lips before snatching a nearby box of tissues to clean me up.

I lay there, sprawled out on the desk, trying catch my breath. These two men acting like they didn't just fuck the same girl silly. I chuckle and rest my face against the surface.

It's not the ending to the master plan I anticipated, but maybe this is better.

— ☠ —

Thank you for reading **Wings of a Devil**.

If you'd like more from this dark and dangerous universe, visit www.lunapierce.com to find other books!

Want to read Johnny and Claire's epic love story about how they overcame the impossible? *Broken Like You*, a gritty contemporary MF romance is available now!

Join June, the seductive take-no-shit vixen, and her brutal mafia men in *Untamed Vixen*, a dark mafia reverse harem romance.

Sign up for the Luna Pierce newsletter at http://lunapierce.-com/subscribe!

ALSO BY LUNA PIERCE

Sinners and Angels Universe

(Dark romance with MF, RH, and MFM)

Broken Like You (Standalone MF)

Untamed Vixen (RH Part One)

Villain Era (RH Part Two)

Wings of a Devil (MFM Standalone novella)

Ruin My Life (RH Standalone)

Brothers of Sin Series

(MF billionaire romance)

Grumpy Billionaire Bad Boy (Standalone)

Book two (Standalone)

Book three (Standalone)

Book four (Standalone)

The Harper Shadow Academy Series

(Paranormal academy reverse harem)

Hidden Magic

Cursed Magic

Wicked Magic

Ancient Magic

Sacred Magic

Harper Shadow Academy: Complete Box Set

Falling for the Enemy Series

ABOUT THE AUTHOR

Luna Pierce is the author of gritty romance, both dark contemporary and paranormal. She adores writing broken characters you won't help but fall for on their journey to find themselves and fight for what they love. Her stories are for the hopelessly romantic who enjoy grit, angst, and passion.

When she's not writing, you'll find her consuming way too much coffee, making endless to-do lists, and spending time with her daughter and cats in small-town Ohio.

Join the exclusive reader group: Luna Pierce's Gritty Romance Squad

Join Luna's newsletter to receive updates at: www.lunapierce. com/subscribe

If you enjoyed reading Bank's story, please consider leaving an honest review on Amazon, Goodreads, Tiktok, and/or BookBub.